CRAZY CLASSICS

Login: Dracula

Une histoire réinterprétée par

Peter Flynn

et illustrée par Euan Cook

didier

... et encore merci à Soizic Cornet et Caroline Moreau, dont l'enthousiasme et la connaissance des élèves ont aidé cet ouvrage à trouver la bonne altitude !

Direction artistique : Mandy Norman
Maquette intérieure et composition : Becky Chilcott
Édition : Sandrine Paniel
Responsable éditoriale : Catherine Laurent
Enregistrements : Studio Corby

 – ISBN 9782278079438 – Imprimé en Italie
Dépôt légal : 7943/05 – Achevé d'imprimer en février 2017 par Grafica Veneta

paper planes *teens*

Une collection imaginée avec humour, enthousiasme et provocation par Rupert Morgan

Tous les titres que vous pourrez enfin lire en anglais !

Débutant
A1→A2

- What is Brian? *Rupert Morgan*
- Which is Brian? *Rupert Morgan*
- Welcome to Star School, *Michaela Morgan*
- Panic at Star School, *Michaela Morgan*
- Star School on Tour, *Michaela Morgan*

Intermédiaire
A2→B1

- Macbeth and the Creature from Hell, *Roger Morris*
- Romeo and Juliet in Las Vegas, *Rupert Morgan*
- Facebook Dracula, *Peter Flynn*
- Bubonic Britain, *Philippa Boston*
- Deadly Jobs, *Philippa Boston*
- Blitz Britain, *Philippa Boston*
- Killer Sports, *Philippa Boston*

Avancé
B1

- Frankenstein 2.0, *Roger Morris*
- Live Fast, Die Young, *Rupert Morgan*
- Rock Rebels, *Rupert Morgan*

Expert
B2

- The River Killers, *Michael Gregorio*
- After The Sea Rose, *M. F. W. Curran*

Monday, December 14th, 2015

METRO LONDON

FIRE AT MIDNIGHT

Number of deaths unclear as raging fire destroys the fashionable Midnight Hotel.

An uncertain number of people were killed last night when fire ravaged a hotel in central London. It is not clear how the conflagration started, but the damage to the fashionable Midnight Hotel is extensive, with the owners saying that it will cost millions of pounds to restore the historic building to its former glory. The hotel has lately become the

1 Police Deposition

Inspector: Tell me about the fire.

Mina: You won't believe me.

Inspector: Why not?

Mina: You just won't.

Inspector: Let me be clear about this, Miss Murray. You were at the scene of a fire which caused extensive damage to a major hotel in Central London. Several people are missing. We want to know exactly what happened.

Mina: You'll never find them now.

Inspector: Really? We've got all your messages on Snaptalk.

Mina: What messages?

2 Snaptalk Conversation

S **November 4, 2015**

MINA MURRAY

Gender: Female

Interested in: Men

Relationship status:
In a relationship with Johnny

Lives: In West London

Studies: Psychology

★ FRIENDS

JOHNNY

LUCY

ALEX

+ 300 more

★ LIKES

Dancing in clubs ★ Playing the piano

New vegetarian recipes ★ Travel

MESSAGES

Mina: Did you see Johnny in class today?

Lucy: No, not since the weekend. He went to Sleepless with Alex.

Mina: Was Alex in class?

Lucy: Yeah, he ignored me again.

Mina: Ignore him back!

Lucy: Did you see the photos from Sleepless?

Mina: What is Sleepless anyway?

Lucy:

MESSAGES

Lucy: Free bar and free buffet, music sounds amazing. ☺

Mina: Johnny usually texts me every day, but he hasn't returned any of my calls or anything.

Lucy: You're worrying me now! Maybe he's sick.

Mina: No, he'd still call. Tell me if you hear anything, ok?

Lucy: He'll be in touch soon.

Mina: I hope so. Laters.

Lucy: Laters.

Friendship request from

VLAD

+ ADD FRIEND

3 Police Deposition

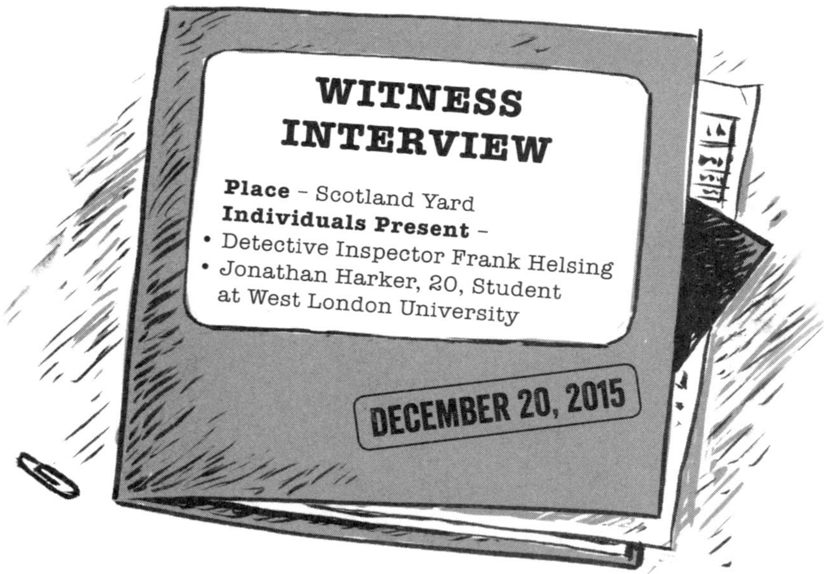

Inspector: 'Sleepless was amazing.'

Johnny: I'm sorry?

Inspector: It's right here in your message dated November 7th: 'Sleepless was amazing', it says.

Johnny: Since when do the police hack into private files?

Inspector: Since a missing person case and a fire in a hotel which could put you into prison for a long, long time.

Johnny: Put me in prison? Why?

Inspector: Tell me what happened at Sleepless.

Johnny: Just dancing. It's a club night[1].

Inspector: 'Sleepless was amazing'. Amazing enough for you not to call your fiancée for a week afterwards? Amazing enough that you went back to the hotel on the night of the fire to destroy it?

Johnny: You can't just put me in prison for some messages on Snaptalk!

Inspector: You're right. We can put *both* of you in prison, you and Miss Murray. She is your fiancée, isn't she – Mina?

Johnny: You're lying.

Inspector: Who's Vlad, Johnny?

[Brief silence]

Johnny: ... you really want to know what happened?

Inspector: That's why we're here.

Johnny: Sleepless... was a regular club night on the fifth floor of this posh[2] hotel in Piccadilly. The DJs are always fantastic. My friend Alex was totally into it[3], and took me along. He was a little drunk that night and we ended up getting into a fight... it was the music, you know? You only get music like that at Sleepless...

1. *Le terme* **club night** *est utilisé pour parler d'une soirée qui a lieu dans un hôtel ou tout autre lieu (mais pas dans un* night club, *c'est-à-dire ailleurs que dans une boîte de nuit).*
2. **posh:** *huppé*
3. **be into something:** like something very much

Inspector: Go on.

Johnny: Alex pushed me and I fell over. I found myself lying at the DJ's feet and... it must have been the lights, but his eyes were... it was like they were on fire.

Inspector: This was the DJ named... Vlad, yes?

Johnny: Yeah... Vlad. He looked angry, and he was strong: he picked me up like I was a baby. I jumped away from him and Alex pulled me away from the mixing desk.

Inspector: But you stayed in the club?

Johnny: Alex wanted to stay. I didn't say anything to him about it, but I couldn't stop thinking about the DJ's eyes. I felt more and more nervous, and I wanted to call Mina, just talk to her. But then I couldn't find my phone. Somebody had stolen it. I got really mad and told Alex I was leaving. So we were just walking out through Reception – and I saw him, the DJ, getting in the lift with my phone! He was holding it up and smiling at me!

Inspector: How did you know it was your phone?

Johnny: I could see Mina's photo on the screen. He wanted me to see it. I was so angry that I walked straight up to him and held out my hand, then I heard the doors closing behind me, and everything went...

[Long pause]

Inspector: Everything went what?

[Long pause]

Johnny: I don't know... it's like a blank!

[Long pause]

Inspector: Do you need a break?

[Recording stops.]

4 Police Deposition

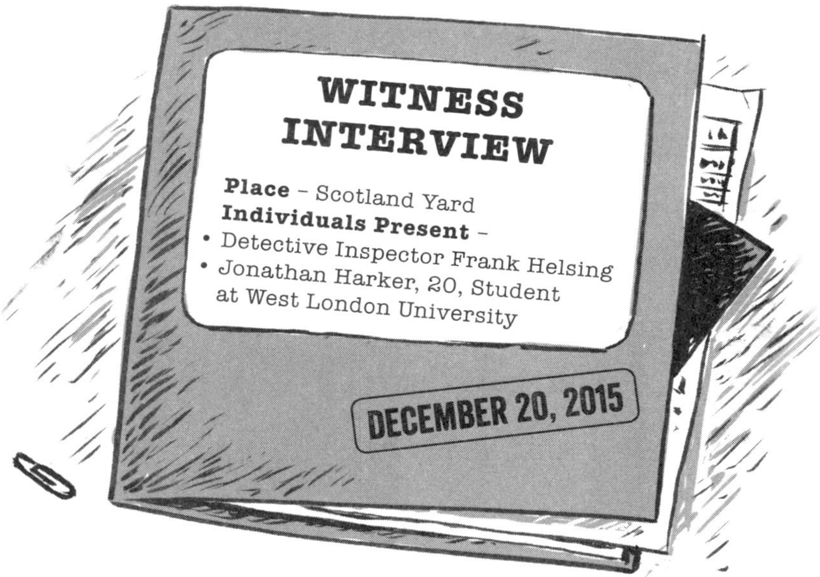

Inspector: So… you were trying to remember what happened after you got into the lift.

Johnny: Yeah… I woke up in a bedroom. It was full of antique furniture like it was about 200 years old, but when I opened the door, I realised I was still in the hotel! It was seven thirty the next evening – I'd slept all day and I felt terrible. I walked up and down the corridor, but I couldn't find the lifts or the stairs – just a lot of pictures and potted plants. I heard music coming from behind

a door, so I knocked. Vlad opened the door. He was very polite – the first thing he did was to hand me my phone.

Inspector: What did he say?

Johnny: 'What a beautiful neck.'

Inspector: I'm sorry?

Johnny: He pointed at the photo of Mina and said, 'What a beautiful neck she has.' I warned him that Mina was my girlfriend, but he just clapped me on the back and congratulated me. It was strange – I felt like the proudest guy in the world...

Inspector: Did you leave at this point?

Johnny: No... he served some vodka for me and we sat in his huge room, talking about London and where I was from. His voice was low... kind of hypnotising... and I heard myself telling him I wanted to marry Mina. I would never normally talk about my feelings to a stranger, but I couldn't stop. He kept looking at me in a strange way, smiling. Then he said we should become friends on Snaptalk.

Inspector: Did you do it?

Johnny: No. I pretended my account wasn't working. Then he said I looked tired and if I wanted I could stay the night in the hotel. I wanted to go home but I felt confused... and then I realised that he was right. I did feel really tired!

Inspector: Did he give you drugs?

Johnny: No – at least I don't think so. I remember walking back down the corridor with him and him warning me to stay away from the other rooms. I asked him why but he just closed the door of my room on me.

Inspector: So you spent another night there?

Johnny: Yes. And when I woke up next morning, there was an amazing breakfast waiting for me in my room. After I finished it, I went out into the corridor, but I still couldn't find the way out. Eventually, I went back to my room and found there was a video console with about a hundred games to choose from. I'd never liked games much before, but these ones were amazing. I just... found myself playing them all day. And, each time I looked outside my room, there would be a plateau of delicious food there.

Inspector: So let me get this right. You're saying that you were kidnapped by a DJ who lives in a hotel and that you spent *three days* playing computer games? No drugs?

Johnny: No! I was happy. I can't remember ever being so happy. I didn't think of anyone, not even Mina. Every night Vlad would invite me to his room for dinner and we'd talk for hours. He was an amazing guy, soft voice, East European, really interesting. Whenever I asked him when I could go, he'd say 'Friend me first.'

Inspector: Why was it so important to him to be friends with you on Snaptalk?

Johnny: He said he wanted to meet all my friends. But I knew he was talking about Mina. And I felt... something terrible would happen to her if I let him near her. Especially after I saw...

[Long pause]

Inspector: After you saw what?

Johnny: Oh god... look, I know what you're going to say, okay? But one night I heard a sound outside the window: a sound of wolves howling[1]. Wolves, in the centre of London! It was crazy, so I opened the window and looked out. I saw Vlad's head looking out of a nearby window. Then he climbed out of his room and he...*crawled*[2] down the side of the building, like a lizard.

Inspector: I see. And you still maintain that you –

Johnny: No! No drugs! I saw it! After that, I was really scared. I was prepared to do anything to get away from there, so the next time he asked me to friend him... I did it. We were out in the corridor, and the second I friended him I heard the 'ting' of the lift doors opening. He just smiled and let me go. I got the hell out of the hotel and ran to find Mina. I had to warn her...

1. **howling:** *hurlant*
2. **crawl:** *ramper, marcher à quatre pattes*

5 Snaptalk Conversation

S **November 9, 2015**

JOHNNY HARKER

Gender: Male

Interested in: Women

Relationship status:
In a relationship with Mina

Lives: In West London

Studies: Psychology

★ FRIENDS

MINA

LUCY

ALEX

+ 100 more

★ LIKES

Traveling in Eastern Europe ★ Arsenal FC

Playing the guitar ★ Hip Hop

MESSAGES

Mina: Johnny, where the hell have you been?

Johnny: Mina, there's a guy called Vlad, whatever you do, don't contact him.

Mina: Vlad the DJ? He tried to friend me.

Johnny: Block him. Don't talk to him.

Mina: Why? What happened?
Is there something you need to tell me?

Johnny: Not here. Not now.
Let's meet tomorrow and I'll explain.

Mina: I'm just glad you're safe. ☺

Johnny: Don't let him in, Mina.
You promise?

Mina: I promise, Johnny.

Johnny: I can't wait to see you tomorrow. Kiss.

[Johnny logs off.]

Mina: Kiss.

[Mina logs off.]

Vlad: Kiss kiss, Mina.

Sleepless
THE MIDNIGHT HOTEL
NOVEMBER 23, 2015
FREE BAR, BUFFET AND BLOODY MARY'S
DJ VLAD/PARTY TIL DAWN
DRESS DARK

6 Snaptalk Conversation

S **November 16, 2015**

LUCY WESTERN

Gender: Female

Interested in: Men

Relationship status:
Recently single

Lives: In West London

Studies: Psychology

★ FRIENDS

JOHNNY

MINA

ALEX

+ 300 more

★ LIKES

Floral wedding arrangements ★

Children – I want to be a primary school teacher!

MESSAGES

Lucy: Are you going to Sleepless? They're promoting it all over Snaptalk.

Mina: Don't go.

Lucy: I've been chatting with the DJ. He sounds sexy. ☺

Mina: Lucy, stay away from him!

[Vlad logs in.]

Vlad: Good evening, Lucy. How are you?

Lucy: Hi Vlad!

Vlad: Hello, Mina. You look lovely in Lucy's album.

MESSAGES

Mina: Lucy, you friended him?

Lucy: So?

Vlad: One week until Sleepless. I'd love you both to come.

Lucy: Sleepless sounds amazing, Min! Let's go.

Vlad: It *is* amazing, Mina. Have you heard about what happened last time? Have a look at these messages:

> **Maria:** Johnny on a bed with three women? Really???
>
> **Lucas:** Three girls! Lucky guy!
>
> **Andrea:** Should we tell Mina about it?
>
> **Stefan:** She won't like it...

7 Snaptalk Conversation

S **November 19, 2015**

SLEEPLESS

Responses to Sleepless invitation:

Lucy, Maria, Lucas, Andrea and Stefan are going to Sleepless

MESSAGES

Mina: Can't wait. ☺

Johnny: Min, I told you not to go! Why aren't you answering the phone?

Mina: It sounds like *you* had fun at Sleepless, so why can't I try it out?

Johnny: That was completely different, Min.

Mina: So it's *true*?!

8 Police Deposition

Inspector: What exactly happened at the hotel that made Mina so furious?

Johnny: Why is that important?

Inspector: Perhaps it gave her a motive to start the fire at the hotel.

Johnny: She was mad at *me*, that's all!

Inspector: What for? What did you do?

Johnny: I... I think it was the second night I was in the hotel. I was looking for an exit when I smelled perfume... a strange perfume coming from a room with an open door. Vlad had told me not to go into other rooms, but I thought someone might help me. There was nobody in the room, but the perfume was making my head turn so I lay down on the bed... I think I must have closed my eyes for a moment.

Inspector: Did you sleep?

Johnny: I don't think so – or not for long, anyway. I woke up because I heard a sound of whispering and giggling*. It was suddenly much darker in the room and there were... three women there.

***whispering and giggling:** *murmures et gloussements*

Inspector: What did they look like?

Johnny: Beautiful. So beautiful. Two of them were in their late twenties, and there was a blonde girl of about eighteen. The two women didn't look at me, they just said 'He's yours' to the blonde. She turned to smile at me and as she came toward me... I found I couldn't move...

Inspector: Really? How convenient.

Johnny: She smelled of perfume and something old and rotten*. Her teeth were sharp like little knives... and as she kissed my neck I felt something cut me. Suddenly, Vlad burst into the room, shouting 'Stop!' and he pulled the blonde woman off me. She said 'But we're hungry, what

***rotten:** *pourri*

about us?', and he placed a bag on the floor. I heard a baby crying... the women went up to the bag, licking their lips, and then I think I must have passed out. When I woke up I was back in my room...

Inspector: And yet you keep insisting that you were not taking drugs at this time? I find that hard to believe. How did Mina react when you told her about this... episode?

Johnny: To be honest, at that point Mina wasn't the problem. It was Lucy.

9 Snaptalk Conversation

S **November 24, 2015**

ALEX HOLMWOOD

Gender: Male

Interested in: Lucy

Relationship status:
[was] in a relationship with Lucy

Lives: In West London

Studies: Information Technology

★ FRIENDS

JOHNNY

LUCY

MINA

+ 56 more

★ LIKES

Grand Theft Auto ★ On-line gaming ★ Kebabs

MESSAGES

Alex: I think Lucy's sick, Mina – she's not answering the phone.

Mina: What do you care? You've been ignoring her since you broke up.

Alex: She's been ignoring *me*!

Johnny: Lucy and Mina went to Sleepless, Alex.

Alex: Seriously?

Mina: Lucy's sick in bed. I think she's got the flu.

Johnny: It's not the flu.

10 Snaptalk Conversation

S **November 25, 2015**

MINA MURRAY

Gender: Female
Interested in: Men
Relationship status:
In a relationship with Johnny
Lives: In West London
Studies: Psychology

MESSAGES

Mina: What is it with you?

Lucy: I couldn't wake up. ☺

Mina: Sleepless...?

Lucy: Lol

Mina: Andrea told me you got hurt?

Lucy: I woke up and there was blood on my pillow. Can you believe that?

MESSAGES

Mina: Did the DJ give you a lovebite?

Lucy: And how. My neck was bleeding. It was a bit scary but it's stopped now.

Mina: You told Alex about it? He's been really stressing out.

Lucy: He's trying to find that DJ. Wants to kill him. Do you know that guy's friended Maria and Andrea as well?

Mina: He moves fast. ☺

Lucy: Sleepless was really bizarre, don't you think? I didn't even like the music much, but I couldn't stop dancing.

MESSAGES

Mina: I didn't trust that DJ guy.
I can't explain it but there's something wrong about him.

Lucy: You believe that crazy stuff Johnny's been telling you?

Friendship request from

VLAD

+ ADD FRIEND

Lucy: It's bizarre, but I can't stop thinking about him. His profile page is completely blank, there's no photos or anything.

Mina: He's nasty, Lucy. Stay away from him.

Lucy: I've got to go.

Mina: You ok? You want me to come round?

Lucy: No, I don't feel well, don't want to give it to you.

Mina: Call me if you need anything.

[Mina logs off.]

11 Snaptalk Conversation

S **November 26, 2015**

MINA MURRAY

Gender: Female

Interested in: Men

Relationship status:
In a relationship with Johnny

Lives: In West London

Studies: Psychology

MESSAGES

Mina: I've been calling Lucy all day and she hasn't answered.

Johnny: That's crazy. Vlad must have put something in her drink

Mina: OK, I'll call her flatmate. Johnny?

Johnny: Yeah.

Mina: This is seriously bizarre,
and it's bigger than I thought, you know..?

Johnny: I know.

Mina: I'm sorry I didn't believe you, about the women and the hotel room, that stuff… I was just worried about you.

Johnny: OK…thanks. Laters.

[Johnny logs off.]

Mina: I love you.

Friendship request from

VLAD

+ ADD FRIEND

[Mina logs off.]

12 Police Deposition

Inspector: This is the security camera film from the Sleepless club night, Miss Murray. Can you explain what exactly is happening here?

Mina: You know what's happening. I'm dancing with Vlad.

Inspector: He's not on the film, Miss Murray.

Mina: No, he's not. And you know why. You know exactly why.

23:58:13

Inspector: That's a little improbable, don't you think?

Mina: He doesn't *ever* show up on video, Inspector! Maria sent me a Flashgram of Lucy that she filmed with her phone. It's the same – she looks as if she was alone, but Maria says Vlad was there, dancing with her! Lucy's head suddenly jerked* to one side... her eyes opened in shock and blood started to run down her neck... I swear to God it's true!

Inspector: Do you still have this video?

Mina: Inspector, do you even know what Flashgram *is*? The video disappears once you've looked at it, so of course I don't still have it!

***jerk:** *tressaillir*

13 Snaptalk Conversation

S **November 30, 2015**

LUCY WESTERN

Gender: Female

Interested in: Men

Relationship status:
In a relationship with Vlad

Lives: In West London

Studies: Psychology

MESSAGES

Mina: I told you to stay away from that guy!

Lucy: He took me out late night shopping and we got the most beautiful shoes, Min! He's such a gentleman, he opened doors for me wherever we went...

Mina: Lucy, he bit you!

Lucy: It was only a lovebite, Min. And he *is* really handsome. ☺

MESSAGES

Mina: I saw a photo of you in the Yoghurt Bar. You've lost so much weight…

Lucy: I never feel hungry any more. When I'm alone, I feel weak, but when I'm with Vlad I feel stronger. Last night he took me to a midnight bookshop in Soho*. And do you know what he said afterwards?

Mina: Tell me.

Lucy: We went back to his hotel, then he held me close and said 'This is your time.'

Mina: 'This is your time…'? What does that even mean?

Lucy: It means he loves me. And he's a great kisser. ☺

Mina: Just be careful, Lucy. You heard from Maria or Lucas recently?

Lucy: I know Vlad's in contact with them. They're his friends. And Andrea.

Mina: No!

Lucy: It's only friending, Mina! Good night.

[Lucy logs off.]

***Soho** is a district in London.

MESSAGES
Friendship request from
VLAD
+ ADD FRIEND

14 Police Deposition

Inspector: And that was the last you heard from her?

Mina: She got sick really suddenly. Her dad took her to hospital but nobody could find what was wrong with her. She wouldn't eat. I saw a photo of her from the Midnight Bookshop... she was really thin and pale. Vlad wasn't in the picture, of course.

Inspector: How did you feel about all this?

Mina: Lucy was my friend! How do you *think* I felt?

Inspector: Perhaps you were jealous of her, for being so close to Vlad.

Mina: Are you crazy? You think I liked Vlad? I thought you said you had read all my Snaptalk conversations!

15 Snaptalk Conversation

S **December 2, 2015**

MINA MURRAY

Gender: Female

Interested in: Men

Relationship status:
In a relationship with Johnny

Lives: In West London
Studies: Psychology

MESSAGES

Vlad: You have such a beautiful neck, Mina.

Mina: Go to hell.

Vlad: I'd love to paint your neck…or make a sculpture of it. Mina in alabaster[1].

Mina: Creep[2].

Vlad: Why won't you friend me, Mina? We can have fun.

Mina: We all hate you, you know. Why don't you leave us alone?

1. **alabaster:** *albâtre*
2. **creep:** *ici, minable*

Vlad: You're too lovely to be left alone, Mina. I'm coming for you: not tonight, not tomorrow, but soon, Mina. Soon.

16 Snaptalk Conversation

S

December 6, 2015

★ **STATUS UPDATES:**

MARIA
♥ In a relationship with Vlad

ANDREA
♥ In a relationship with Vlad

STEFAN
♥ In a relationship with Vlad

LUCAS
♥ In a relationship with Vlad

MESSAGES

Alex: Maybe we should get the police on him.

Johnny: What for? Friending people? Biting? Students do that all the time.

Alex: You know what this looks like. I can't say it because it sounds too crazy.

Johnny: Exactly. No one would believe any of this. All we have is photos of people dancing with the Invisible Man.

Alex: I say we go to the hotel and face him ourselves.

Johnny: No way. I'm not going back there.

[Mina logs in.]

Mina: Alex. It's Lucy...

Alex: What's wrong?

Mina: They couldn't do anything for her.

Johnny: What?

Mina: They couldn't do anything for her. Lucy died in hospital this morning.

17 Police Deposition

Inspector: Lucy died, and yet you still friended him? Why?

Mina: He just... *persuaded* me: it wasn't my fault, it was Sara, my flatmate. I'd told her not to let anyone in. Then there was a knock on the door of our apartment at midnight. I heard her talking downstairs, low voices. Sara came running upstairs, really excited, and told me that Johnny was here to see me.

Inspector: Why didn't Johnny call to say he was coming?

Mina: I didn't think, I just said, 'let him in.' When she went back, there was nobody at the door. I asked Sara what the man looked like and she said, 'Tall, dark hair, pale and handsome.'

Inspector: But Johnny's blond.

Mina: Exactly. I phoned him, but he didn't answer. So I just went back to bed and tried to sleep... but I couldn't.

Inspector: Why not?

Mina: Something woke me up... there was whispering... something in the room. A cloud of mist at the end of my bed... and then I saw Vlad in a dark suit. I wanted to run, but I couldn't move. I was frozen to the bed. He came over to me and kissed my neck: a long, slow kiss. Then he unbuttoned his shirt and ran a fingernail across his chest and cut himself.

Inspector: Are you quite sure it wasn't a dream?

Mina: That was no dream, Inspector! He pulled my mouth toward the blood and I... I had to drink. I couldn't stop myself, it was the most delicious thing I'd ever tasted. He talked to me all the while, saying 'This is your time...' He promised me a new life, a world of sensation and pleasure... and then Johnny and Sara came running up the stairs and burst in the room.

Inspector: And how did Johnny react when he saw you with Vlad?

Mina: Vlad was gone. He'd just... disappeared.

18 Snaptalk Conversation

S **December 13, 2015**

JOHNNY HARKER

Gender: Male
Interested in: Women
Relationship status:
Lives: In West London
Studies: Psychology

MESSAGES

Mina: What do you mean it was her?
It must have been someone else.

Alex: Five people said they saw her
in the club, dancing on the bar.

Johnny: That doesn't even sound like
Lucy, Alex. She was never a party animal.

Alex: They say she bit the barman.

Johnny: Alex, she died a week ago!
It's *not* her!

MESSAGES

Alex: They tried to take photos of her, Johnny. She didn't show up in any of them. You know what she is now. We've got to go to the hotel and stop this.

Johnny: I'm not going back to that hotel.

Alex: We have to, Johnny.
The only way to free Lucy is to kill Vlad. We have to do it.
Johnny?
Johnny?
You still there?

Johnny: Mina's just woken up.
She's scared. She says she can sense him thinking of her. Like he has a connection to her mind.

Alex: What are you talking about?

Johnny: I haven't told you yet
– Vlad got into her flat last night.
He bit her.

Alex: Is that where you are now?
Stay there – I'm coming round.

19 Police Deposition

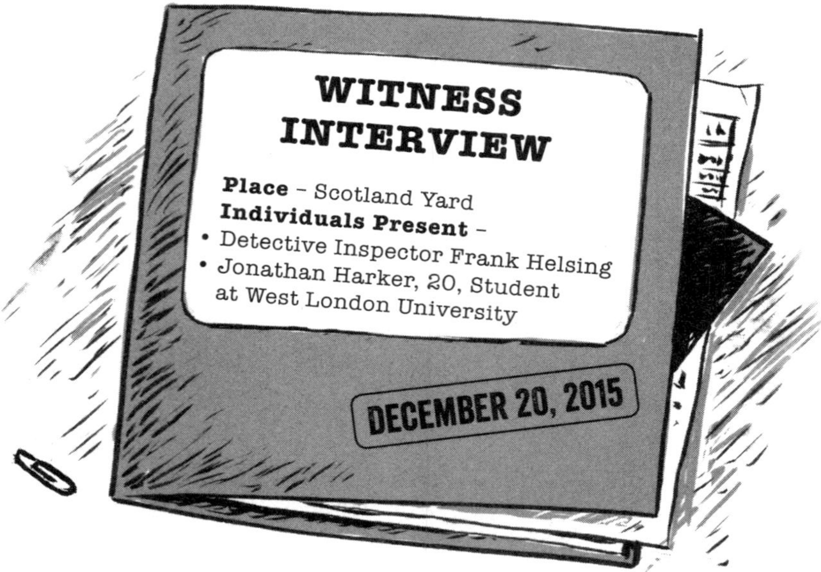

Inspector: Tell me about the fire.

Johnny: The three of us went to the hotel – Alex, Mina and me. It was around eight in the morning, and Mina was wearing this big hat because she said the sun was hurting her eyes. None of us had really slept all night...

Inspector: What was your plan at this point?

Johnny: Mina had told us that she had a connection with Vlad. She could feel where he was because... he had infected her. But she said this meant she could take us to the 13th floor.

Inspector: Do you realise that, like many London hotels, the Hotel Midnight *has* no 13th floor, Mr Harker? People are superstitious about these things.

Johnny: I know. But when we got into the lift, Mina touched the panel between the buttons for floors 12 and 14, and I saw the number 13 *appear*, Inspector!

Inspector: And Miss Murray just... knew how to do this?

Johnny: She knew everything! She knew exactly where to find Vlad. She closed her eyes and said '1314. He's in room 1314...' The corridor was dark when we got there, and there were no light switches, so we used the torches on our phones to see where we were going. We were as quiet as possible, nobody saying a word, but she must have... I don't know... sensed our odour, I suppose. The door to her room just opened by itself as we walked past, and there she was...

Inspector: Who?

Johnny: Lucy, of course!

20 Police Deposition

Mina: I'd never seen Lucy look so beautiful... she held out her arms to Alex and smiled, saying, 'Kiss me, Alex'. Before we could stop him, he walked straight into her arms. As she kissed Alex on the neck, I heard doors opening all around us. There were familiar voices in the darkness – Maria and Andrea, Lucas and Stefan, all calling out to us. They sounded hungry.

Inspector: Was this Vlad among them?

Mina: Yes, his room was next to Lucy's. He looked delighted as he appeared – he knew we were surrounded. This was exactly what he wanted. But then there was a cry from Alex – Lucy was biting him now! He pushed her away with all his force and she fell back against the window, pulling down the curtain as she fell. Suddenly the room was filled with sunlight. She burst into flames and ran from the room, screaming in agony.

Inspector: And that was how the fire started?

Mina: Yes! Lucy ran all over the place, panicking as the flames consumed her! She took hold of Vlad and screamed for help. His clothes caught fire and he pushed her away, falling back into the room, which was when Johnny jumped on him with the knife.

Inspector: And what about the other... people that you mentioned?

Mina: Maria and Andrea jumped on Johnny like animals, biting at his neck. I tried to pull them off while Johnny struck at Vlad, over and over again, with the knife. Finally, he plunged it into his chest, fixing him to the floor, and Vlad just... fell into dust.

Inspector: But you were still being attacked by the others?

Mina: No – they stopped as soon as Vlad was gone. They just seemed to be confused suddenly, and I knew

they were free of Vlad's control. It was too late for us to stop the fire, so we ran before the fumes became too thick. Alex found a fire escape and we all got out together, a little burned and out of breath, but alive...

Inspector: And you're sure of all this, Miss Murray? You're quite sure of everything you have told me? It's all... a little incredible, isn't it?

Mina: I know. But even you can't deny one thing I told you is true, Inspector.

Inspector: What's that?

Mina: I said that you wouldn't believe me.